BIGFOOT STORIES 4

By Jada L. Roberts

TABLE OF CONTENTS

Forward

By Jada L. Roberts

Greetings Bigfoot believers, skeptics, adventurers, Bigfoot hunters, eye-witnesses, and mystery seekers

Since writing my first book series "Sharing the Mountain with Bigfoot", I have received many emails, letters, and phone calls from other eyewitnesses who wanted their stories to be told, and they wanted me to share their stories.

This is the fourth book in the series of "Jada L. Roberts Bigfoot Stories" and certainly not the last. I have many people wanting me to write about their stories and I have enjoyed every minute of it.

As I said in the last three books of this series, if you have a story that you want told but want to stay anonymous, please email me at www.jadalroberts07@gmail.com and reach out to me. I will help you in any way.

So, get relaxed, turn down the lights and be prepared to read about some very interesting stories that may make you wonder what could be out in your back yard. But be warned, you may lose a little sleep and jump at everything that goes bump in the night.

*Please note that some names and places have been change to protect the people who were willing to share their stories.

Forgotten Mountain

John's Story

My story begins in the early spring of 2002. I was 47 years old, married, had a great job, and lived in Moab, Utah. There were so many things to do around Moab. On the weekends my favorite thing to do was go hiking, camping, and exploring the State Parks that were nearby. For many years on Friday afternoons after work, my wife and I would pack an overnight bag and go camping on BLM (Bureau Land Management) land and hike up mountains and visit the many parks such as Dead Horse Point State Park. Of course, no one can forget Arches National Park is only five miles away from Moab and that was my favorite place to go.

One bright and beautiful Friday morning as I arrived at work, I began to think of where my wife and I could go for the weekend. As soon as I reached my office, I began searching for a nice campground and a place to explore that we have not explored yet, (there were little to no places around Moab that we haven't explored) or haven't in a long time. As I studied the surrounding area, to my surprise, I found a beautiful place where we could go that was secluded that I thought my wife would love. I had noticed a sullen change in my wife as she seemed a little withdrawn and not interested in the things she used to love to do. I thought that she just needed a break from her everyday life and I wanted this weekend to be special. I began planning a romantic trip for the weekend that I thought would be memorable for the both of us.

As my work day ended, I could hardly wait to get home and tell her to pack her bags for an unforgettable weekend. As I drove into the driveway, I noticed another vehicle parked in my parking spot. As I parked behind my wife's car, I realized that our only child had come to visit us. Dustin (our 26-year-old son) had graduated from college and moved to San Diego to pursue his career. He did not visit us very often so it was a happy surprise to me that he was here.

I quickly opened the front door and was expected to see happy faces and receive hugs all around, but all I heard were muffled voices coming from the kitchen. I followed their voices and stepped into the kitchen to see my wife and son packing our belongings into boxes. Neither one had heard me come in so when they noticed I was standing behind them my son came to me, gave me a hug, and walked out of the kitchen. It was just me and my wife standing there looking at each other.

I did not have to say a word for she began to explain what was happening. She told me that she no longer was happy with me and she was moving to San Diego with our son. She handed me a stack of papers and walked out of the kitchen to join my son. I looked down at the papers and prayed to God that it was not a divorce decree. But to my horror, it was. My happy life just crumbled into a million pieces.

After that moment everything was a blur. There was no use trying to reconcile with her for her mind was made up. She moved to San Diego, we sold the house, split everything, and went our separate ways. But that did not mean that I was over the ultimate shock of my life. My life was turned upside down. I did not know what I did to deserve this. My wife (now ex-wife) and my son were not in my life anymore. Both did not want any communication with me. It traumatized me so much that I had to get away from Moab. I could not live in the same place that I had lived for so many years, built my life with my wife and raised my son in and be happy after both had left. I could not visit the same places that my family visited and feel comfortable. It was too much to bear.

I thought long and hard of what I wanted to do since I was alone and single. I decided that I did not want to work at the same job any longer and be near anyone until I was able to get over the divorce and losing my family. So, I decided that I would retire early. I took out my 401k (happy that my ex did not want half of it) and with the money I got from selling our home (my half), I decided to do something that I never thought I would ever do. I bought a pickup truck with a camper top on the back and converted it into a small RV. I decided that in order to be alone and do what made me happy, I would travel to other states and do all the hiking, camping, and exploring that I wanted to do. There was nothing holding me back and no one I had to make happy. It was just me.

I loaded up my truck and hit the road. The farther away from Moab, the better I felt. For months I felt free and visited the states of Montana, Wyoming, Colorado, Oregon, and Idaho. The depression and initial shock of what had happened started to wane and I began to feel a little like myself again. My energy was coming back and I learned how to rock climb. With all the massive mountains located in the western United States, I wanted to try something new. To my surprise, I learned rock climbing quickly. I also made a few friends along the way. But my favorite was still hiking up the mountains, along with camping for free in the BLM lands.

It was in Idaho where I had the scare of my life. I heard of a beautiful remote and scenic lake in the forgotten mountains of East Central Idaho. The high desert mountains. It was told that it was the most beautiful place on earth and I needed to see for myself. So, off I went to the high desert mountains.

****

The road to the parking area and trail head was very rugged and dusty. It meandered through a deep canyon then opened to the parking lot with a lone building that read "Men and Women" restrooms. I was the only person there (which I liked very much) but it was early in the morning when I got there and I expected that the place would get a little more human activity throughout the day.

The lake I wanted to walk to was about 2 ½ miles away that I would have to go up and over a ridge to get there with a 1000 feet of elevation gain.

I parked and stepped out of the truck. The first thing I saw was how beautiful my surroundings were. It felt like I was in a big bowl with the mountains as the sides. The chill of the early morning breeze stung my exposed skin but I knew that the day would warm as I walked toward the lake.

I locked the doors of the truck and made my way toward the trail head. I zipped the windbreaker jacket up to help with the cold wind that whipped through the canyon as I followed the well-maintained path that ascended the mountain. I found my walking comfort zone and prepared for the long hike to the lake.

Nothing was extraordinary about this hike so far. The views were beautiful but I have been to many beautiful places. But as my mind began to think of other things besides walking, suddenly I looked up and noticed a cave close to the trail. Since it was accessible, I knew I had to explore it. The only thing between the cave and the trail was a small downhill slope and a steep climb to the cave.

After climbing the steep hill, I entered the cave, (more like a large, deep overhang) and noticed it was not anything that special, but I knew that Native Americans had used it in the past and there was something strange about the area. A chill went up my spine and I felt as if I was being watched. It spooked me a little as I explored more of the cave. As I was ready to leave, I noticed on the far side of the cave there seemed to be a large pile of branches and leaves on the ground like a nest of some sort. I walked toward it to get a better look when something glittered in the sunlight that caught my eye. On a half-buried boulder there lie a golden Cross pendant. As I picked it up to examine it, I realized it was attached to a golden chain. I didn't put much thought into it for many people lose jewelry all the time and I thought someone had been exploring the cave in the past a lost it. I put the necklace in the same hand as my walking stick and continued exploring. I walked closer to the nest but suddenly, I wanted to leave. Not because something had frightened me but there was a rancid smell close to the so-called nest. To me it smelled of burnt hair and feces, and the closer I got to the pile of leaves, the stronger it was. I was ready go to continue my trek toward the lake. I turned and made my way back to the trail and continued. I made way up the ridge when I realized I still had the cross pendant and necklace in my hand. It had wrapped around my walking stick. I did not want to back track and replace it but I made a mental note to put it back where I found it on the way back to my truck. I swiftly put it in my front pocket and forgot about it.

As I followed the trail up the ridge, I came upon the remnants of an old cabin right beside the trail. I thought how cool it would be to have lived in this remote, beautiful place. I explored the area for a few moments and then continued my hike toward the top of the ridge. It took about an hour to reach the top and as I stood there, I was amazed of the beauty of the place. The view was breathtaking!

After about another thirty-five-minute walk I made it to my destination. The beautiful lake. I took my backpack off and sat down on the ground to relax and prepare food. After finishing my lunch, I laid down on the hard ground with my backpack as a pillow and stared at my surroundings. On the opposite side of the lake were trees and rock mounds and in the distance were snowcapped mountains. I also loved the fact that I was the only person around to enjoy this beautiful place.

In my relaxed state of mind, I must have dozed off. For the next thing I remember, it was two hours later and it had turned cold and snowing. My body was getting cold, especially my feet and I was ready to go. I knew I had a long trek ahead of me back to the truck so I grabbed my backpack and started on the trail. I quickened my pace and climbed the ridge to the top. I kept a steady pace as I passed the old cabin that I explored earlier and made good time descending toward the trail head. My mind was occupied with other things besides walking. I knew I needed to find a good camping spot on BLM land before dark. As my mind was pre occupied with other things, I never realized that I was close to the cave until that same putrid smell hit me in the face. The smell was coming from the cave and was so strong that I had to cover my nose and mouth with my hand. I kept my pace as I passed the cave. I glanced up at it and thought I saw a black figure standing close to where the huge nest was. It looked as if the figure was swaying from left to right as it watched me walk past. I thought my mind was playing tricks on me as I quickened my pace and hurried down the path toward my truck.

In my heightened awareness, the path seemed a lot longer on the way back as it did earlier. But finally, I made it to the trail head and the truck in sight. Still yet, not a single vehicle in the parking lot except mine. It was so quiet and peaceful that I had forgotten about what I thought I saw on the trail as I stopped to take in the beauty of the area. I finally had my fill of scenery and hopped in the truck. I still had to find a camping spot for the night and it was getting very late.

After driving around for a while, I found my camping spot. I parked my truck in a canyon called Skull Canyon and it was a beautiful, rugged, tons of cliffs, remote place. The road was full of ruts, big pot holes, and in some places, loose sand that was deep enough to get my truck stuck in. It was hard getting to this camping spot so I knew I would not have many campers (if any) around me. I figured I would be all alone and that was how I liked it. As I explored around, I looked up into the canyon walls and noticed a few caves and arches that were visible from my camp spot. A little eerie but beautiful at the same time.

The sun was fading fast and my stomach was talking to me. I realized how hungry I felt as I quickly gathered the small grill out of the back of the truck and fumbled around in the ice cooler until I found the large piece of sirloin steak I had bought earlier when I stocked up on supplies for this trip. I wanted to fill up on a nice dinner and have a relaxing night so I could get up early in the morning to go explore the next day. I had planned on driving to a well-known area with the main attraction was a waterfall, but since I had found this canyon, I decided I would stay a couple days at this location and see what I could find in the surrounding area.

It was fully dark as I sat near the small campfire. With my belly full of steak and instant mashed potatoes, I stared up at the night sky and was awed by the beauty of the night. The stars dotted the clear skies and the breeze felt so fresh and pure. The temperature was around 40-degrees Fahrenheit but dropping quickly. With a breeze that would blow through the canyon ever so often, I knew it would be too cold to stay out by the fire for long but I wanted to enjoy the night if I could. As I sat there by the fire and took a sip of hot tea I had brewed, suddenly, a breeze whipped through the canyon and the hair on the back of my neck stood up and a chill went down my spine. Within that breeze, I smelled same putrid smell that I had encountered earlier by the cave on the trail. At that moment, I was ready to crawl into my sleeper camper and go to bed.

I folded my lounge chair and leaned it up against the side of the truck, opened the driver side door, grabbed the keys, locked the doors, and walked behind the truck, lifted the tail gate and slid into the bed of the truck and onto my air mattress. I locked the camper window lock, turned on the battery-operated lamp and began to undress. I wanted to get out of the dirty clothes that I had hiked in all day. As I pulled my pants off, everything in my pockets emptied out onto the bed. As I looked to see what had fallen out, there was the gold chain with the cross pendant that I had found in the cave. I picked it up and put it on a small ledge beside the bed and did not think any more about it. I snuggled into the covers and readied myself for a good night sleep.

With cold temperatures and snuggled into thick blankets, I fell into a deep sleep. I had slept for a few hours when I awoke and realized that I was very thirsty. I fumbled around in the same cooler that I had earlier for my dinner and found a bottle of water. I took a couple large sips and returned the bottle back into the cooler. As soon as I closed the lid, suddenly the loudest noise came from the side of the truck. Something big had hit the passenger side of the vehicle! It hit so hard that the whole truck shook! It startled me so bad that my heart began to race as I quickly dressed in the same clothes I had on earlier and grabbed a flashlight. I searched around for any kind of protection I had. At that moment, I felt angry at myself for the only thing I had for protection was a baseball bat. I made a note to make sure from then on to have a weapon in the camper for nights like this.

I grabbed the bat and reached for the keys to unlock the camper window to step out of the truck. but before I had time to open the window, suddenly, a loud and unnatural scream echoed through the canyon and I froze in place. I literally could not move a muscle as the scream went on for about fifteen seconds or longer. When the scream was over, the silence was deafening. The only thing I could hear was my heartbeat beating loudly in my ears.

I sat there for a few moments and I thought that maybe the ordeal was over and the creature that was around me had move on and out of the vicinity. I finally got the nerve up to look out the camper window to see if I could see anything. The windows were tinted very dark so I did not know if I could see out of them. But of course, being dark outside and the tint on the windows, I just saw my reflection in the window. I knew I had to open the tail gate and step outside of the camper to know if I was alone or something was waiting for me to come out.

I sat there for a few more minutes as I nervously reached toward the latch to open the tail gate. At that moment I wished I had some way to get into the cab of the truck without having to get out of the camper, but the old truck I had decided to use did not have a back window to open to slide into the front. I had to get out and walk around to the front door to get in. I was ready to leave the area as fast as I could for, I did not feel safe.

After a few more minutes of silence, I realized I had over reacted and thought that the loud scream could have been a large cat that were native to the area. I also knew that if it was, the animal would be long gone and it felt safe enough to get out of the camper.

I reached for the latch and opened the top back window. I cautiously climbed out of the camper and instantly felt the cold night air. I quickly shown my flashlight in the vicinity of where I thought the scream had come from but the small light was too dim to see very far. I decided to use the truck's headlights to have better lighting. I reached back in the camper to find the keys. As soon as I found them and had them in my hand, another loud guttural scream came barreling down the canyon and echoed off the walls. Frightened, I slid the keys off the air mattress and noticed something else had slid with them and landed on the ground. I looked down and saw the cross pendant and gold chain laid by my feet but I had no time to pick it up. I raced around the truck to the driver's side door to unlock and jump in the seat. I fumbled around as I tried to unlock the door and in a panicked state, I dropped the keys in the sand. With flashlight in hand, I found them quickly and unlocked the door. I jumped in and started the engine, turned on the high beams and put the truck in drive. As soon as I grabbed the steering wheel and about to drive away, suddenly, my blood ran cold and I froze in place. I could not move a muscle. My body was so tense that it hurt. All I could do was let out a small whimper as my eyes were glued to the creature that stood bipedal in the beams of the truck's headlights.

It seemed that we stared at each other for hours (but, it was for but a minute or two) as I watched the large creature sway from side to side. I noticed how long the arms were (and it was covered with long hair and all the other descriptions that I had read about in books) and knew exactly what I was staring at!

A BIGFOOT! It had to be! But this creature was different from what I had read about. In the headlights that shown so brightly on it, I could see distinct features. In my heightened awareness, I could see that the beast stood about six feet tall, broad shoulders, small waist, and the hips were wider than the waist. The body was covered in hair except in one spot. The chest/breast area! As it swayed from side to side, I could see that the breast would also sway and were quite large. Dumbfounded and still in a panicked mode, I questioned what I had in my sight. I questioned if this was reality or was it just a dream. I questioned everything in existence at that moment in time

But as we stared at each other for a good while, I calmed my nerves and knew that if she wanted to attack, she would have done so already. But what did she want from me? Food? Water? I had both and would have given all of what I had to her. But I would have to get out of the safety of the cab of the truck and go to the back to get it. I did not want to try that and risk my life. All I wanted to do was to get out of the area and drive as far away as possible.

As I slowly moved my hand up to the lever to put the truck in drive, a flash of remembrance came to me from my hike from earlier that morning. The trail... The cave... The awful stench... The golden cross necklace...

The golden Cross necklace? Surely Not? Had this Bigfoot like creature followed me to take back what I had stolen from it from the cave earlier in the day?

As the creature stood in beams of the headlights, I remembered that the necklace had fallen to the ground as I grabbed my keys. It was directly behind my truck!

I slowly put the lever in reverse and backed up far enough that I knew I was safe and for the necklace to be in between me and the Bigfoot. I watched as the creature took a step forward but never moved her eyes off me. With my nerves in total shock, I watched as she slowly moved toward me. But I knew she was not wanting anything to do with me, it was what I had stolen from her. She wanted what was rightfully hers.

It seemed a lifetime (it was just a few moments) before the Bigfoot reached the necklace that laid on the ground between me and her. But as soon as she was on top of it, she slowly bent down and picked the necklace and cross pendant up, stood back up and swiftly moved out of the bright beams of my headlights and into the darkness.

For a moment I still could not move. I could not see far enough out in the distance to know where the creature had gone. My imagination got the best of me as I thought that maybe it was right behind my truck and would launch a surprise attack on me. My nerves shot up once again as I slammed the lever back into drive, found the dirt road, and high tailed it out of the area. I could not get out of there fast enough! But finally, I found the paved road, turned onto it, and headed back into the nearest town to spend the rest of the night in a Wal-Mart parking lot. There I knew I was safe for the night where there were other people around and no large creatures lurking around my truck.

In conclusion, that night had changed me forever. Now, I do not go hiking or camping alone, which I am happy to tell that I do not have to. I met my beautiful fiancé and now she goes with me. I also have upgraded my RV/truck to a class A diesel RV so I will never have to leave the vehicle to drive away if need be. And, I have met many friends along the way and now live a very happy life.

There is one very important advice I will leave here:

Never take anything out of the woods that does not belong to you. You never know what may come looking for it! I learned my lesson the hard way.

When the Sun Went Down

Kevin's Story

I have a very large family. So large in fact, that if we go anywhere, we usually take up the whole area and have the place to ourselves. What I mean about that is if we went out to dinner at a restaurant, we would take all the seating in the whole place.

We are also a very close-knit family. The "fam" as we call ourselves, consists of aunts, uncles, brothers, sisters, cousins, etc, etc... not just immediate family members. (I promise this will make more sense later in the story.) We are so close that we all live blocks away from each other. We see each other daily and our get-togethers are every other Saturday.

The one family member I was very close to was my uncle Bill. When planning a family get-together, uncle Bill would suggest that we all go to a park or to a campground so we could relax, go fishing, bike ride, and just have fun, instead of having to make reservations to accommodate the large number of members that attended. I thought that was a great idea because, for a fourteen-year-old, I really did not like getting all dressed up to go to a fancy restaurant, wait for all to be seated, then wait some more to order our food, and then wait more for the food to be delivered, and so forth. I thought it was a waste of "wait" time when we could be out in the great outdoors doing fun things like fishing, hiking, or just relaxing while "waiting" on dinner to be served. But most of the family enjoyed all the "wait" time and wanted to go into the city for our gatherings. My uncle Bill and I were outnumbered when it came to voting on going to a park or camping for our gathering versus making reservations at a fancy restaurant every time. That is, until one weekend, we were not outnumbered and most of the family voted to side with Uncle and I.

I was still in a somewhat shocked state when I came home from school on a Friday afternoon and my mother asked me to help her pack our camping supplies in the trunk of the car for a weekend getaway with the Fam. I was so happy that my Uncle Bill's persistence had paid off and we were finally going camping instead of the dreaded restaurant scene. I happily joined my mother and sister in gathering the tents, sleeping bags, blankets, and totes filled to the brim with cooking supplies and food. I had no idea where we were going camping at but my mind was filled of all the fun activities that I imagined we would be doing. I wanted to take my fishing rod, bike, hiking shoes, swimsuit, and anything else that I thought I may need on this trip. But to my dismay, I knew that I could not bring most because we had no room in the car to put them. But that did not stop me from trying.

With the last tote of cooking supplies carried out to the car, I looked down the street to my uncle Bill's house and noticed he had hooked up his bass boat behind his truck. That is when it fully hit me. I was ecstatic! We were really going camping and I knew we were going to have the best weekend ever! I also realized there was enough room in the boat to put my fishing supplies. I was beyond excited!

I squeezed the last tote of food supplies into the trunk and took off running down to my uncle's house.

When I reached the driveway to his house, I stopped running and noticed that uncle Bill was coming out of the front door with a big smile on his face. He looked so happy and stress free. Not like other times when he would come home from work as a manager of a manufacturing company. He looked so tired and stressed. But not this time, he looked like a whole new person.

Heavily out of breath from running from my house to his, I asked if I could put my fishing equipment in the boat. He probably knew we had no room in the car for my mother was his sister and he knew all too well that she would try to pack the whole house just for a weekend getaway. He let out a jolly laugh and told me that there was no need to bring my fishing gear, he had it all taken care of. I let out a sigh of relief and noticed I had never seen Uncle Bill so happy and full of energy. His eyes sparkled while we planned our weekend of what we wanted to do. We knew that maybe the men in the "Fam' would want to fish but we knew that Grandma, mother, sister, and nieces would want to do other things. So, Uncle Bill and I visioned what we would do when we arrived at our camping spot.

That night I stayed up late. I wanted to make sure I had everything I wanted to take all packed up. Even though this was just a weekend camping trip, it seemed to me like a long vacation. I could not remember the last time my family had taken a vacation so I was sure to make the best out of this camping trip. When I finally laid down and fell asleep, I began to dream. A nightmare would be a better term. I guess the camping trip had led into my subconscious mind for in my nightmare, we were already set up at a camp spot and enjoying the nature around us. We had just finished dinner and were relaxing by the camp fire, when suddenly, a loud scream came from the woods that startled everyone. A scream I had never heard before. The next thing in my dream was I was running down a narrow path away from something huge that was chasing me. My heart was beating rapidly and I could hardly breathe. My legs felt like a ton of bricks as I tried to run faster. The thing that was chasing me looked like a half man, half bear- and it was gaining on me! as I turned around to see if I was out running it, I noticed that it was upon me and reached out to grab my arm. Panicked, I tried to run faster, but I tripped over a log in the path and fell on my back. As I looked up, all I could see was a bright light in my eyes and a massive arm reaching out to grab me. Suddenly, I awoke and noticed that the bright light in my dream was the sunlight streaming through my bedroom window and into my eyes. I let out a long sigh as I rolled over to face the wall, then I realized it was daylight and time to get up and get ready for the awesome weekend we had planned. As soon as we were all in the car and leaving the house, the dream/nightmare was all forgotten about and the anticipated fun weekend had taken its place in my mind.

While on our way to the campground, I never knew where we were going, and for some odd reason, I never asked. I just enjoyed the ride out of the city and into more sparsely populated area. The four lane roads turned into two lanes, and trees replaced building on the side of the narrow road. I noticed that it was taking a long time to get to our destination, and I began to get bored of riding in the cramped car. My little sister (twelve years old at the time) began annoying me with her "want to play a game?" questions and constantly talking about unimportant things that only mattered to – no one. She would only talk about things because, just like me, she was bored and ready to move out of the cramped back seat of the car we were in.

Just when I thought I could not take any more of my sister's annoyance, the stuffy air that came from the car's air vents, the cramped back seat, and the boredom that overwhelmed me, I asked the most famous question that children ask their parents. I leaned up and took a deep breath and asked "Are we there Yet?" in a somewhat desperate tone of voice.

As soon as the words left my lips, I noticed the turn signal suddenly flicker on and we began to turn onto a gravel road. I looked out my side window and saw a sign that read "Mountain Pass Campground" and I knew we had finally made it to our camp. I felt a rush of excitement as I reached for the door handle to open as soon as the car came to a stop. But the gravel road was so long and curvy that I had loosened my grip on the door handle and turned around to see the rest of the family that had followed us. I counted six cars behind us and Uncle Bill and Auntie Janet led the pack with the boat in tow. In all, eight vehicles on a small dusty gravel road did not help the stuffy air in the back of our cramped car. But we were almost there!

A lifetime later (it would seem), I stood where our tent later would be placed and took a deep breath of fresh air that filled my lungs. I could hardly wait to go exploring in the campground. As I looked around though, I noticed there were no other campers in the small campground. Even though we were a big crowd, I surely thought that other humans would be around to enjoy the great outdoors and be camping also. I glanced around more and noticed that many, if not all, of the camping spots were overgrown with tall grass and weeds. It looked as though no one has occupied any of the spaces in a very long time. Even the gravel road had tall grass growing in the middle of it. My heart sank a little when I saw that the campground was not how I had pictured it, but when I saw the beautiful lake at the end of the road, my mind changed in an instant and I knew we were going to have the best weekend ever!

When all the tents were erected and the paths were cleared to them, my cousin Tim and I met at the end of the gravel road where Uncle Bill had placed his boat by the lake. We were ready to go fishing. I wanted to go as soon as possible for it was getting late in the evening and I knew that Uncle Bill would have us back on shore before nightfall, but we did not have to wait long for Uncle Bill was ready to go also. We all climbed into the boat and Uncle started it up and we headed toward the middle of the lake. It did not take long to be in the middle and Uncle Bill killed the motor and we came to a stop. We readied our fishing poles and began fishing. I do not know how long we were out there in the middle but we never caught a fish and we all were ready to move to another location.

Uncle Bill started the motor and slowly moved toward the bank and out of sight of the campground. We thought that fishing in shallower waters we may have a better chance of catching a fish and maybe enough to grill over the camp fire. We found our place and set up for fishing. Uncle Bill and cousin Tim had cast their line out before I could get mine baited. When I was ready to throw my line out, I moved to the front of the boat so that my line would be near the water's edge and close to small trees that had fallen into the water. I had hoped that was where the fish may be hiding.

I carefully aimed where I wanted my bait to land and with a steady hand, I reared back and flicked the line toward the fallen trees. I watched as it landed in the exact spot I wanted it to.

I slowly began to reel in the line when suddenly, something big hit the water right beside the boat and made a huge splash right beside me! The splash was so large that it soaked the right side of my pants. I quickly turned to see if anything had fallen off the boat, but nothing had. Nothing that heavy could have possibly fallen off the boat.

I turned to Uncle Bill as he asked me what had happened and if I lost anything when again, something hit the water near the boat and make another huge splash. This time it was closer to the back of the boat where Uncle Bill was sitting. Startled, Uncle Bill yelled out "Hey, stop that! You are scaring the fish away!" as he thought it may be someone in our family trying to scare us when suddenly, another big splash occurred at about the same place as the last one hit.

That is when I got a little spooked. I saw on my uncles face a look of fright, or concern. Without saying a word, he quickly reeled in his bait and started up the motor. He put it in high gear and raced toward camp. I barely had time to reel in my cast before we were ordered off the boat and go straight to our campsite. With the way he was acting, I left everything on the boat, jumped out, and ran to my campsite. Tim was right on my heels and followed me. When we arrived, we plopped down by the camp fire and told my dad what had happened.

Dad stood up and told us that he would go help uncle Bill with the boat. I watched as he swiftly walked the small path we created to our campsite, turned right onto the gravel road,

and headed toward the lake. As I turned back around to face the camp fire, mother came out of the tent with her hands full of food and motioned me to come help her. She handed me a casserole dish and Tim and I followed her out of our campsite and to the made-up community campground. We met the rest of the "Fam" there as they prepared a feast for us all. Dad and uncle Bill came in just in time as dinner was served.

The sun was setting about the time we finished dinner and about the time for the adults to sit around to socialize. The women would be in one group and talk about what shows they watched during the weekdays and gossip about other people from their church. The men would form another group and talk about random stuff like football, the latest tools, and machinery. The younger children would be running around playing games and annoying their mothers. But, Tim and I (the only teenagers in the family at the time) would suffer from boredom and have nothing interesting to do. That is until Tim had an idea that I agreed to.

"Let's go explore the campground" he said with excitement in his voice.

It was not completely dark and I knew the campground was very small. I thought we could explore it and be back before the sun went down. Even though it was dusk, I did not think much about how fast it gets dark at dusk.

"Okay, let's go" I replied, as I stood up and waited for him to tell his dad what we were doing. I noticed that his dad gave him something as Tim swiftly put it in his pocket.

I did not think much about it as we headed down the path toward the gravel road. Instead of going toward the lake, we went the other direction from where we came in. I wanted to see how many campsites there were and if any other campers came in after us.

As we walked the gravel road, the light from the sun faded fast. I looked up to the sky and noticed the stars were shining brightly and there were no clouds in the sky. The moon was on full display and looked beautiful in the cloudless sky.

As we walked, and as I assumed, there were no other campers around. As a matter of thinking, I never saw a ranger station, gift shop, or any kind of small building when we came in to the campgrounds. That got me thinking, if anyone ever visited this place and how did our family make reservations or book a campsite here?

While my mind was in another place, Tim's mind must have been too. He silently walked beside me with his eyes to the ground. I nudged him gently as he came back to reality. We both laughed and stopped walking. We looked around and realized it was completely dark and we had walked much farther than we wanted to. A little fear took hold of my mind as we both turned around to walk back to camp. We held the same speed of walking as we had when we were going away from camp and began small talk with each other.

We were in deep conversation and enjoying our time out on the gravel road. The full moon and cloudless skies gave enough glow for us to see where we were going and to follow the road back to our family. We were talking about a girl that Tim had a crush on when suddenly, we both stopped in our tracks and an overwhelming feeling of being watched took over us.

I did not know what to think about it for that was the first time I had ever felt something like that. My heart began to race and I felt edgy. I looked over at Tim and saw that he too had felt the same as I. His body shivered as he reached into his pants pocket and pulled out a small flashlight. He flicked it on and shined it all around us. As we were hoping, we did not see anything unusual, so, he turned the light off and we began to quickly walk back to the safety of our camps. But as soon as we turned a curve in the road, we once again stopped in our tracks!

A feeling of helplessness washed over me. I was frozen in place and I held my breath as to hold on to it like it was my very last! I could feel Tim's whole body shivering next to me.

Right in front of us, in the middle of the road, between us and the safety of our campsite, stood the largest creature I had ever saw!

At first, I could only make out the shadow of the creature. The moon glow was the only light we had. I saw a small head, very large shoulders, the waist was slim, and very muscular legs, especially the calves. The only other thing that frightened me the most was how tall it seemed to be.

As I stared at the beast in front of us, I heard a faint whimper come from Tim. I turned my gaze to him as he slowly pulled the flashlight out of his pocket, pointed it to the creature and with shaking hands, clicked the button, and the beam of light shown the creature's face.

I had only about a second to get a glimpse of what it looked like. As soon as the light hit the creature's face, its large yellow eyes lit up and a deep growl bellowed out toward us. We both were frozen in fear, when suddenly, Tim let out a high pitch scream, dropped the flashlight and sprinted off the gravel road and into the woods, away from our camp! In a split second, the yellow eyed, large beast also ran into the woods in the same direction as Tim!

I stood frozen in place as I could hear Tim's screams with each step he took. When I realized that the monster must be giving chase to Tim, I snapped out of my panicked mode, picked up the flashlight and ran toward camp, all the while screaming as loud as I could.

I did not have to run very far before I saw in front of me about five beams of flashlights coming my way. Our loud yells and screams had alerted our family as they ran toward me. When I saw the lights were getting closer, I ran faster as the tears streamed down my face. My legs felt so heavy and weak as I tried to reach them as soon as I could. When I heard my dad's familiar voice call out my name, my legs collapsed and I fell on the ground. As they reached me, I was so much in shock that I could hardly tell them what had happened. The only thing I could stutter out was "Help Tim!" as I pointed back down the gravel road from where I came.

My uncle Bill, grandpa, dad, and other males in the family began running down the road to where I pointed to go rescue Tim. Mother finally made it to where I was, helped me up and walked me back to camp. I tried to tell her and my aunties what had happened but I was still in shock from what I saw and I was worried sick about Tim. I hoped and prayed that he was not hurt and Uncle Bill would find him soon.

When I finally told my story to mother and others who gathered around me, I heard auntie Janet exclaim, "oh my, that sounds like a Bigfoot!" as she paced back and forth around the campfire.

"Janet! Don't say that in front of Kevin" mother barked, "besides, you don't believe in Bigfoot, do you?"

Auntie Janet turned to my mother as a frightened look washed over her face "yes, I do" she quietly replied.

Tears rolled down my cheeks once again as I realized that Bigfoot was not a made-up creature after all. It was real! And Tim was out in the woods being chased by one! I just could not believe what I had just saw as I impatiently waited for my cousin Tim to come back to camp. I could hardly wait for this nightmare to be over.

As we sat (some paced, some sat in their vehicles) around the campfire, I noticed how eerily quiet the woods were. I could not hear any nocturnal insects, frogs, or any animals of any kind. All I heard was the crackling of the fire that we kept lit. It seemed that the fire was our only protection and to keep us from losing our sanity as we waited for the men to bring back Tim.

I began to calm my nerves as I stared at the blazing campfire. My body stopped shaking and I leaned back in the chair to try to relax. I slumped down in the chair and laid my head on the backrest and closed my eyes. Immediately, the nightmare I had the night before flooded my mind. It was so vivid. I remembered some creature chased me and I could not run fast enough. I remembered in the dream that I was on a path in the woods trying to get away. But what I remembered the most was the creature that chased me in the nightmare, resembled what the same thing Tim and I saw standing in front of us on the gravel road. And soon had chased Tim in the woods!

My body began to tremble as panic sat in again. I raised my head up to fight the chill I had when mother wrapped a heavy blanket around my shoulders. I tried to stand up to see if I could see if uncle Bill and others were bringing Tim back but I was so weak and every muscle in my body ached. My breathing was labored as I tried to calm my nerves, when suddenly, I heard Auntie Janet yell out, "here they come! I see their flashlights!"

Stiff muscles and all, I jumped up and ran to them. As I came closer, I realized Tim's father was carrying him in his arms and it seemed he was not moving. My heart pounded in my chest as I approached them and noticed that Tim was breathing. He also had bloody scratches all over his arms and face. His clothes were stained with dirt and one of his shoes was missing.

His father rushed past me and put Tim in the back seat of his car. Without saying a word, he jumped into the driver's seat, started the car, and drove out of the campground. I watched as the tail lights faded into the distance before I turned to my uncle Bill for answers.

"Pack up, we're leaving tonight" he said as he rushed to his truck to retrieve his boat and dismantle their campsite.

My parents were busily throwing everything we had at our campsite into the car. I quickly fell in place and helped my mother load up all the totes once again into the car, all the while my little sister clang onto mother like her life depended on it. Then I helped dad tear down the tents we had carefully erected earlier that day. I could hear the rest of the family muttering and tearing down their campsites too. All the lights were on in the vehicles to have as much light as possible. It was chaos all around. But finally, everyone's campsite was cleared and we followed each other out of the campground and soon was on the road back home.

The next day, uncle Bill and I went to visit Tim in the hospital. As we walked into the room, my uncle Tom and aunt Verdie, sat next to the bed. Uncle Tom told us that he would make a full recovery. He was in a state of shock. The scratches were from all the sticks and briars that he had ran into while he ran in the thick woods. I was so relieved to hear that my best friend and cousin would be alright. While Tim slept, uncle Bill and I quietly slipped out of the room and he took me to my favorite ice cream parlor.

For years, no one had spoken a word about that night. Tim made a full recovery but would never mention what had happened to him in the woods. I tried to bring up the subject once or twice, but he never wanted to talk about it. So, I gave up asking and just had to live without knowing the whole story.

Until the day came when he suddenly wanted to tell me what had happened.

We were in our late twenties when Tim decided it was time to share his story. Remember, this incident happened when we were both fourteen years old.

Throughout the years, Tim and I stayed close to each other. We both finished school, had great jobs, and married with a son. My son at the time was two years old and so was his son. We wanted our sons to grow up just like we did. Best friends and family.

One night, Tim, his wife and son came over for dinner. While his wife and mine gossiped in the kitchen, Tim and I went into the den to watch the children play. That is when he decided to tell me the story that I wanted to know for so many years.

"I had an overwhelming feeling of being watched. That is what spooked me first. Then I noticed the woods being unusually quiet. That put me on edge. I was ready to run back to camp when I remembered the flashlight my dad gave me before we left. I wanted to keep it on for the rest of the way back to camp but was afraid that if there was a bear or something in the woods, the light would attract it. But, when we turned the corner and there was this huge creature in the middle of the road, I froze. I didn't know what to do. All I thought about was maybe if I did shine the light in its eyes, it may have scared it and would run away. Boy, was I wrong! When I saw the yellow eyes, my fight or flight sensors came on and I took flight. I panicked and took off running, thinking I could go around him in the woods. That was stupid.

"I remember just running as fast as I could in my panicked state, when I realized I was on a narrow path leading to... I do not know where. I thought it would lead back to camp but it was led me deeper in the woods. I kept running and as I looked behind me, I saw the creature closing in on me. Panic set in again and I tried to run faster but I knew I could not out run this massive thing. Then I tripped over something and planted face down in the dirt. As soon as I rolled over, a bright light shown in my eyes and an arm reached out to grab me. I began to fight off whatever was trying to attack me, but as I struggled, I heard my dad's voice as he tried to calm me. I knew then I would survive. I must have hit my head hard enough to black out for a little while. My dad took my arm, lifted me, and carried me all the way back to camp. I did get a good look at the monster that chased me" he said and looked at me knowingly, "Bigfoot! They are real. But I do not talk about what happened to me because I still have nightmares about it from time to time. And I do not want people to think I'm crazy. My wife already thinks I am" he finished with a nervous chuckle.

Finally, he told me the story of what happened. But then it hit me. My dream the night before the camping trip! It was almost exactly what he just told me. I still remember that nightmare to this day. So vivid and every detail. Very strange indeed.

That is the conclusion of my story except to tell from that day forward, the family never went camping again and we were happy to go into the city for our weekend get-togethers.

Thank you for reading,   Kevin

School Project
Nathan's Story

It all started in high school. I met a girl (Heather) in History class and we were teamed up with a school project. At first, I did not think her and I would be a good fit to work together. I was head quarterback of the football team and she was the smartest girl in class. My girlfriend was the captain of the cheerleading squad and the most popular person in high school. She was also in my history class and I wanted to be her teammate. But the teacher knew that and wanted to separate us for she wanted me to pass the class. We all knew that if I was paired with my girlfriend, we both would not have finished the assignment.

Every day, I would protest so much that it became embarrassing for the whole class and especially for Heather. At the time, I did not care. My girlfriend was teamed up with another player on my football team and it seemed they were getting too close and I became jealous of them. I did not like for my sweetheart to be close to any other guy. The more I thought about it, the angrier I became. So much so, I threatened the other guy in front of the class and I was sent out. I only accepted defeat when the principal told me if I kept on with this behavior, I would be kicked off the football team.

Football was my whole life. I could not get kicked off the team. I worked so hard to be in the position I held. I had to calm my nerves and team up with a girl I had never spoken to or given a minute of my time to. I only knew her as the smart girl that no one talked to.

Heather was a very quiet girl. She wore large round glasses and put her hair up in a bun on top of her head. Being very petite, she would slip in and out of class like a ninja and no one would take notice of her, and at that time, I did not want to get to know her, nor work with her on an assignment. But I had no choice, I had to pass this class to stay on the football team and the only way to do that was to work with Heather on the assignment.

The day came when the teacher asked everyone to get with their assigned partner to begin working on the assignment. I glanced at my girlfriend and noticed that she jumped up to go sit with her teammate. She was so involved with him that she forgot that I was in the same room. My blood started to boil but I had to calm myself down. I slowly rose from my desk and made my way to the back of the room where Heather sat with her head down, staring at the instructions in front of her.

I plopped down beside her but she never looked up. To get her attention, I cleared my throat and shuffled in my chair.

Finally, she took notice and looked up at me. Her beauty took me by surprise. Bright, sparkling blue eyes shown through the big round glasses, soft brown strands of hair fell loosely around her round face with smooth tan skin, and as she smiled, those full lips parted and revealed the most perfect teeth.

I sat there for a moment in total silence. I could not believe that the nerdy girl that everyone said was the most unpopular girl in school was so beautiful. I guess she had noticed that I was in shock and asked me if I was okay. I snapped out of the daydream that started to form in my head and came back into reality. I had to gather my senses and glanced back up to where my girlfriend was. I did not want her to see me staring at another girl. Of course, she did not. She was too much involved in her teammate. But somehow, at that moment, it did not bother me as much as it had been.

I collected my thoughts and became the "stud" I portrayed to be. I looked at Heather and told her that I did not want to take much time on this assignment and wanted to be finished quickly. I was not interested in this project, and I was just waiting for school day to be over so I could go to the field to practice my sport.

She took out a note pad and we worked in silence. When the class bell rang, she silently slipped out of her desk and headed for the door. I jumped up and headed toward my girlfriend, who was still sitting in her chair beside the other guy. Both never heard the bell ring and were deep in conversation with each other. I quietly walked out of the classroom and headed toward the football field with my mind clouded with the thoughts of – not my girlfriend. But of Heather.

Following weeks went by and I acted the same as customary. Cold to Heather and jealous of my girlfriend and her new friend. I noticed that my girlfriend had pulled away from me somewhat and when her friend would come around, she would tell me she had to discuss the "project" with him and leave me standing alone. That made me beyond mad. But, as the days went by, I began not to care as much as I could hardly wait to go to history class to sit by Heather. To my surprise, I began to think of her more than I did my girlfriend. So much so, that when it was time to go to class, my hand became clammy and my heart felt that it would beat out of my chest. I would have dreams of her and even in football practice, I would be thinking of her. It was very strange for my girlfriend was also beautiful and every guy in the whole high school wanted to date her. But I had the privilege of being her boyfriend.

One day after practice, I looked up in the bleachers where my girlfriend always sat to wait for me to take her home, but she was not there. She told me that she was going shopping with her friends after school and I did not have to drive her home. I was not used to that. I had always taken her home after school or practice and I felt all alone. But somehow, I enjoyed it. I went to the locker room and changed back into my school clothes. When I came to the locker room door that pushed outward, I would always push hard on it so it would fly open and hit the wall. That day was no unusual day. As I approached the door, I stiffened my arm and pushed hard on the door. As soon as I could see the hallway leading outside, I noticed a figure right beside the door walking the same direction of the swinging door. I tried to stop the collision of the door and the person but it was too late. All I heard was a huge thump and books falling to the concrete floor as the door came back and barely missed my face.

I quickly stepped out of the locker room to attend to the injured victim that lay on the floor. When I bent over to help her up, to my horror and surprise, I found myself staring deep into Heather's big blue eyes! Suddenly, guilt swept over me as I tried to help her off the cold concrete walkway as she tried her best to push me away. I knew I had hurt her for I really put some effort in pushing that door hard. I almost could feel her pain as I watched her stand up and rub her forehead with her hand.

I could never apologize enough as I picked up all the books I had knocked out of her hands. I knew she was mad and I expected a good chewing as I turned to hand her things back to her. But as soon as I turned around, I was caught off guard when I looked down and she let out a small chuckle. I was so relieved that she was alright and was not mad at me. After all, it was a mistake. A mistake that I would never want to do again. But a mistake nonetheless.

I had to smile back a her as her beauty shown through the pain she obviously hid. For the first time in years, I was taken aback and speechless. But then I heard her let a small giggle as she looked down and pointed at my crotch area to let me know something was not exactly the way it was supposed to be. I quickly looked down and noticed that in my hurried state of getting dressed back into my school clothes, I forgot to zip my jeans and I was on display for the whole world to see!

Embarrassed, I frantically zipped up as I watched her walk away. As soon as I could I caught up with her and asked if she needed a ride home. I was very surprised when she immediately said "sure" as we turned to walk toward the parking lot and straight to my car. I opened the car door for her and watched as her petite figure slid into the seat.

She gave me directions to take to her house. As we drove passed the town square, we were so deep in conversation that I did not realize that we were way outside of town and into the woods. The road became narrow and the trees on both sides were closing in as if we were driving through a tunnel. Soon after, she pointed up ahead to the right and said to turn off onto a sparsely gravel road. I did as she requested and drove about a half of a mile up, hitting every pot hole on the semi dirt road until we reached an old two-story wooden house with a big wrap around porch. I thought the house had to have been built in the 1800's but it had a unique feel to it. Very charming.

"Would you like to come in and meet my mother?" she asked with a smile and a sparkle in her eye.

"Sure" I replied, but with hesitant start. "But what about your dad? Will he be upset with a guy he had never met bringing you home?"

"It's just me and my mother here" she sighed as she opened the car door and slipped out.

I killed the engine and stepped out. A soft breeze hit my face as I inhaled the fresh countryside air into my lungs. Wow, what a place! I thought as I followed her up to the large steps and onto the huge front porch.

The front door squeaked loudly as we entered in. The smell of freshly made dinner and the soft glow of the light made the large room feel inviting and comfortable. I felt right at home instantly.

Heather shuffled me to the kitchen where her mother was preparing dinner table and introduced us. What a wonderful lady. She invited me to stay and keep them company as we had a full course meal. I enjoyed it so much that time had slipped away and before I realized, it was around midnight and I knew my parents would be very worried about me.

We said our goodnights and I stepped onto the porch. When the door shut and I was out in the front lawn by my self, a strange feeling washed over me. I really could not figure it out at the time but it put a chill through my body and I raced to my car and quickly started the engine. I felt very anxious and could hardly wait to get back into town and closer to my house where there are plenty of street lights and familiar territory.

I finally made it off the gravel road and onto the tunneled paved highway that led back into town. It was still very dark and my high beams were illuminating both sides of the road. I began to relax enough to turn on the radio. As soon as my right hand left the steering wheel to reach for the radio knob, suddenly, my high beams flashed onto something beside the road and in the corner of my eye I thought I say a huge hand go past my passenger side window! Startled, I quickly looked into the rearview mirror to see what I almost hit with my car, but I saw nothing. I slowed my speed for just a few seconds, then thought better of it and accelerated full speed ahead. I had to get out of these woods and fast!

Before long I pulled into my driveway as I saw the front door open and my mother stood on the porch with her hands on her hips. I knew I would hear how much she had worried about where I was and to never do this again. I would hear the same words just about every Friday and Saturday night.

As I laid in bed, all I could think about was how much I had enjoyed being with Heather and her mother. And how much I liked the old house in the woods. What I could do to help fix up all the loose boards and help around that old wooden home. Even though it was a little creepy out in those thick, dark woods, the place seemed to have drawn me in. I wanted to go back as soon as possible. But as soon as I closed my eyes, I remembered the drive back on that dark road, and what was the large hand-like image that passed by my window?

****

The following weeks went by and my life had changed drastically. Yes, I still had football practice and games, but instead of being around my girlfriend all the time, I hardly noticed her. And she also pulled away from me and was always with her partner or with her girlfriends. I would pass her at lunch and go sit next to Heather, but she not once stopped me from doing what I wanted to do. Also, I noticed that more people were sitting at our table with Heather and I and were talking more to her than me. I could not help but notice that she looked happy with her new found friends. It made me happy also.

Almost every day after school and practice, I would drive Heather home and we would work on our project. Her mother would have dinner waiting for us and we all enjoyed each other's company. I made sure to leave the house before sundown and be out of the woods before dark, but since it was nearing the end of the school year, the days were getting longer. But I always had that same weird feeling every time I drove down the gravel road and onto the pavement. No matter the time of evening.

We had finally finished our project and handed it in to the teacher. I was happy to have made the grade so I could stay in my position as the lead football player, but also sad that it had ended for I thought Heather may never invite me back to her house and the time we spent together may be over. When I entered the class, I sat in my assigned seat closer to the front of the class while she sat in the back. I wanted to move my seat closer to hers but I knew that was impossible. The teacher would not let that happen. After class, it seemed like we all were back to normal, we all got up and left the class without speaking to one another and I headed toward the locker rooms to dress for practice.

Out on the field, I thought of nothing but the game. I practiced hard and when the final play was over, I began to walk toward the locker rooms when suddenly, I looked up and saw Heather sitting on the bleachers where my ex-girlfriend used to sit while she waited for me to drive her home. My heart skipped a beat as she gave me a small wave and a smile. I rushed up to her and told her to wait for me and I will gladly take her home.

We arrived at her house and it was the same as usual. Dinner waited on the table and we all chatted while we ate the most delicious meal. Afterwards, we all went into the large cozy living room and relaxed on the sofa. Usually at this time, Heather and I would work on our project, but since that was completed, I decided that we should do something else beside just watch the reruns on tv. I knew what movies were playing at the theater (my dad owned the theater, plus many other businesses in town) and I thought it would be a good idea to take her.

As we were leaving for our date night, she kissed her mother and we walked toward the car. The sun was setting and I began to walk toward the car when suddenly, that same odd feeling rushed over me and I stopped in my tracks. I looked around and tried to investigate the woods but the brush was so thick I could not see through it. I also noticed Heather as she passed me with her eyes pointed to the ground and not saying a word. She just got into the car and shut the door. I jumped in the driver's seat and started the engine. All I wanted to do was make this night memorable for Heather.

After date night was over it was time to take her home. I dreaded the drive down the narrow-tunneled road but I felt at ease with her next to me. She kept great conversation and I hardly thought about the creepiness of the area. It seemed like just a minute had passed by when we made our turn on the gravel road and up to the house.

I parked the car and turned off the lights. That is when I realized how dark the place was. I could hardly see the house. Every light in the house was off and the only light source was the moonglow (which was not very bright) I reached for the door handle to get out when suddenly, a loud, high-pitched scream came from the woods follow by a three very loud knocks that came from behind the car.

Stunned and a little shaken, I turned to Heather for answers. With eyes wide, she raised her hand and grabbed mine and told me to just get out slowly and walk to the house.

Without saying a word, I followed her instructions. I slowly slipped out of the car and met her in front of it and grabbed her hand and we walked to the front porch. I could hardly wait until we were safe inside. When we finally opened the door, I swiftly shut the door and moved far away and into the kitchen.

The house was pitched black and I could not see anything in front of me. I wanted to ask why the house was so dark but I was freaked out too much to say anything. I just stood the in the middle of the kitchen as I waited for something to happen. I thought maybe one of the ladies would turn on the lights but it never happened. it seemed like an eternity before I heard any noise.

My eyes were getting adjusted to the dark when suddenly I saw a bright beam of light from a flashlight that Heather had turned on. She made her way to my side and was about to say something when suddenly, once again, a loud scream came from outside in the woods. But this time, it was closer to the kitchen window where I stood! I panicked and let out a scream myself for I did not know what to think about it all. I was already creeped out by the place and now out in the woods there was some animal whose screams were so loud that it echoed throughout the land.

The dark house, the loud screams coming from outside close to the house and Heather trying to calm me and telling me to be quiet, what was going on?

Finally, Heathers mother opened her bedroom door and flipped the switch to the hall light. It was dim but at least I could see my surroundings and note what the girls were up to. When I stood up to walk toward them, I noticed a baseball bat in the corner of the room. I rushed over and grabbed it and I felt the adrenaline flow through my veins. I braved up and thought to myself I would protect these ladies from the animal that was outside. I also thought that we were safe inside the house and if something tried to get in, I would take care of it.

The strange thing was, I noticed that Heather and her mother was not that scared as I first was. I could not understand that these petite women were not afraid of an unknown creature that close to their house, that made loud guttural screams, and whistles and other strange noises that I could not understand an animal could make. I would soon find out.

I gripped the baseball bat tightly with both hands and walked toward the front door when Heather stopped me.

"Where are you going?" she asked in a whispered voice.

"I'm going out on the porch to see what is out there" I said as I placed my hand on the door knob.

"NO! just wait a few minutes" she replied as she motioned me away from the door.

As I turned away from the door, suddenly, I heard a heavy footstep up onto the porch. The old wooden planks creaked and with each footstep, it seemed that the planks were about to break. I tightened my grip on the bat as I painfully heard the footstep come closer to the front door. I knew that it sounded like a very heavy person was walking on the porch and I readied myself for whatever was to come.

With bat drawn, I waited anxiously by the door but the footsteps stopped and it sounded like what or whomever was on the porch had jumped off with a loud thud.

I slowly turned around to look to see where Heather went when suddenly, the whole house shook and the woods came alive with loud screams, whoops, and what sounded like tin plates clinging together! Shocked and terrified, I ran into the kitchen and found Heather and her mother at the kitchen stove pouring liquid, vegetables, and other edible things in a huge pot. I thought what were they doing? They could not possibly be wanting to cook at a time like this! Was I going crazy?

The loud commotion coming from outside was deafening as I ran over to them and asked the obvious question.

"What are you doing"? I yelled anxiously as my fight or flight sensors kicked into higher gear.

"It's for them" Heather replied as she hurriedly put the lid on the huge pot of soup and waited for the liquid to reach a boiling point.

"Them? Who's Them?" I frantically wanted to know.

"You will find out in about five minutes" mother chimed in "you will help us place this pot on soup on the back porch"

I couldn't help to notice that both Heather and her mother were not that frightened as I was. They calmly stirred the soup as the yells and screams became louder and the sticks and small rocks pelted the house. I was terrified and knew that something was amiss and not natural was happening. I never had heard such a commotion in my life and I knew the wildlife around here could not make these kinds of sounds. The only large wild animals we had in the woods were black bears and I know they could not make the sounds that were heard.

Heathers mother stood up from the kitchen table and picked up a couple of pot holders and handed one to me. She motioned to the back door as she lifted one side of the heavy pot. I fell in place and took the other side of the pot and slowly made our way to the door as Heather quickly opened the door. As soon as the door opened, the woods became silent. All I could hear was the creaks from the old planks as we stepped out on the back porch. We put the heavy pot down and I could not resist to look around to see what was making all the noise. I noticed Heather and her mother went back inside but did not close the door. They waited for me in silence and did not ask me to come in right away.

The light that shown through the kitchen windows illuminated the lawn well. I could see all the way to the tree line to the back of the lawn. As I strained to look beyond the tree line and through the thick underbrush, I noticed movement in the trees. My heightened sense kicked to a higher gear and that's when it happened.

As I scanned the back lawn, suddenly, a huge, massive creature stepped out of the thick woods and into the dim light. My heart skipped a beat and my blood ran cold! It just stood there looking at me as I looked at it. I could not believe what I was looking at. It had to be at least nine feet tall, had short brown hair all over its body, very muscular, and very wide shoulders. But what had me frozen in place was the yellow glowing eyes! It seemed to hypnotize me to where I could not move! And I had a ringing in my ears. I just stood there and could not take my gaze off this creature!

A few minutes went by (but seemed like a lifetime) the ringing in my ears finally subsided and I heard Heathers voice from behind me. I quickly snapped out of the shocked stupor and I realized what I was looking at. I did not believe they existed but I was looking at one in front of me. A Bigfoot! A real Bigfoot!

When Heather came back onto the porch and softly grabbed my arm to guide me back into the house, I stopped at the door and turned to look once more. I watched as the huge creature slowly walk up to the porch, grabbed the pot, and slowly walk back into the forest and disappeared. But I noticed something else too. Before the Bigfoot picked up the pot full of food, it left something on the porch. I could not make out what it was and I was not going out to see what it was. All I wanted to do was to pick up my things and leave as soon as possible, and be at my house in town where there are no large Bigfoot creatures around. But that meant that I had to leave the safety of the house and drive down the creepy little gravel road, down the spooky tunneled narrow paved road to get to town. I decided to stay with Heather and even though I was the one that was terrified, I wanted to make sure they were safe also.

After about an hour after everything had calmed down, Heather and her mother explained to me what had really happened.

"This happens about two times a week" Mother started off

"We moved here about three years ago and immediately we knew we had visitors. At first it scared us badly but we realized what was going on. When I knew that they were not here to harm us, I began to watch them. I had planted a garden out in the back lawn and they would come and take my vegetables but would leave me a gift for them. Some gift were pretty little rocks, some were twisted tree limbs and some were not so pleasant like small dead animals, but to them those were gifts also. So, one day, I had a lot of soup left over that Heather and I would not have eaten and I sat it out for them. I didn't know if they would take it but they did and since then, well, you see what happens. They love the hot food and I enjoy the gifts they bring." She finished with a shrug.

"Is that safe though" I asked

"It has been so far" she replied as she stood up and said her goodnights and walked back to her bedroom, shut the door and left Heather and I alone in the large cozy living room.

That was years ago and I still remember it well and there is a reason I remember it.

After high school, Heather and I got married and we moved into the old house that she shared with her mother. I remolded the house and built an extra room for mother to live in. She was so happy when we told her we were expecting our first born and then told us to slow down when we announced our second child on the way. She lived with us until 2013 when she passed away in her sleep. Heather and I, along with our children lived in the old house for twelve years before we sold it to move for a better job and a better life out west.

As for our visitors, they would visit us about two times a week and we fed them the soup they loved and they would in turn give us gifts. The visits stopped the exact day that Heathers mother passed away. It was strange, but we never saw them again.

Thank you,

Nathan

The Farmer

Pete's Story

I'm not a big talker, so I'll get to the point. I spend all day everyday out in the fields on a tractor tending to my crops. I have about one hundred and fifty acres of land, so not too large and not too small. I get up in the early mornings and don't come home until after dark. I don't have anyone to keep me company all day so I have a lot of time for myself. If I am working my fields and it's not raining, I am happy.

My wife and I live in a two-story farm house that was built in the late 1800's. It is a beautiful house that demands attention quite often. So, if the rain runs me out of the fields, I have plenty of projects to keep me busy for a while. I will keep my location private because I don't really want many people come stomping around my property for what I'm about to tell you. With all that being said, I wanted to share my story with someone that is not from around my location and I thought this was the best way to do it. Here is my story.

I woke up early one morning with the smell of freshly brewed coffee and the distinct smell of bacon frying in a cast iron skillet. My wife had already gotten out of bed and made her way to the kitchen to prepare breakfast. This particular morning was not unusual for my wife and I had been on this farm for twenty-two years and every morning, like this one, was routine. She woke every morning, cooked breakfast, and I would eat it, kiss her goodbye for the day and go work in the fields until dark. I would come in from a long day as she had dinner prepared when I walked into the door. I would eat, kiss her goodnight and fall into a deep sleep and repeat the next day. That was our life and I could tell that my wife (Martha) seemed to be getting tired and restless. I knew this would be a tough life to get used to when we bought this farm back in 1999 but she had agreed for she fell in love with the house. Martha never complained about anything. But the little hints about going on vacation to the beach were getting more frequent and telling me that we had not had a vacation in more than twenty years, I saw her point. We needed a vacation. We just needed to wait until after harvesting.

The year this incident occurred was in 2005. I had planted soy for the season and I was just waiting for harvest time. I had a special surprise for Martha for her birthday. Her birthday was in late September and I wanted to take her on a much-needed vacation. As much as she had taken care of the home and me, she really deserved a long vacation. I could hardly wait to go myself and just get away for a little while.

About the land. The land that I have is very flat so it's easy to manage. I could see from one end to the other when I planted soybean. They are smaller plants and easier to grow. But, in the middle of the field, there stands a large hill that is covered with trees. I sometimes climb to the top of it and have a look around my property. I can see the farm house, along with my neighbor's house and farmland. Sometimes I wish it was not there but nature wanted it to be so I had no choice but to work around it. It does block the view to the other side of my field when I am in the back lawn of the house. But I have become used to it for it has been there since I've owned the property.

It was finally harvest day. I was anxious to get started and get it finished as soon as possible. I knew as soon as I was finished, I would have a good payday and all my hard work would seem worth it. I rose from the comfort of my bed, ate breakfast, kissed my wife goodbye and started the old tractor up and moved toward the field. I drove toward the field as I scanned my surroundings. The dew on the plants were glistening from the morning sun and I thought that was the prettiest thing to see in the field. When I got to the edge, I began to roll over the first row of soy when suddenly, I noticed movement around the big mound that was in the middle of the field. I stopped the tractor to see what or who it was. As soon as I reached for the door handle to step out to get a better look, I saw what I thought was a man in my field. I became angry toward that person for not respecting my wishes as I had "no trespassing signs" posted everywhere around my property, I slung open the door and slid down the tractor. I ran as fast as I could toward the person, yelling to get off my property! But as soon as I about half way to the mound from my tractor, I stopped in my tracks! The creature that I thought was a person suddenly stood up and let out a loud yell!

Goose bumps ran all over my body and I was frozen in place. My heart raced as I could hardly breathe in the crisp morning air. I was in full shock mode as I stared at this creature. It was all I could do to keep my knees from giving out as my legs became weak.

Here I was in the middle of my soy field, with no weapon or anything to protect me, staring at what we call a Bigfoot, which was about twenty yards from me. All I could do was pray that I may have a chance if it decided to charge after me was to make it back to the safety of my tractor. But as huge as it was, I don't think I could out run it. All I could do was pray.

As I stood there, I noticed that the Bigfoot started swaying from side to side and not making a move toward me. I did not want to make eye contact with it so I just stared at its massive, hairy body. With my heavy breathing, I could only smell the fresh morning air, but when the wind changed direction, a smell of rotten flesh mixed with dirt and skunk hit my nostrils and I had to hold my breath so I would not lose my breakfast. It was nauseating.

We both stood there for a while just staring at each other when suddenly, I saw movement behind the creature. As I looked closer, a smaller Bigfoot came out from behind the larger one. I was shocked! A baby Bigfoot? Was this a mama and a baby Bigfoot in my field? I did not notice any feminine features of the larger one but I also wasn't looking. But after seeing the small one, I relaxed a little and decided that I would very slowly walk backwards toward my tractor.

With each step backward, I kept full attention on the creatures. They did not make a move and finally I made it back to the safety of the large tractor. I watched as the large creature took the small one by the hand and both walked toward the end of the field and disappeared into the woods.

I started up the tractor and finished my chores for the day. But I never let my guard down just in case the Bigfoot wanted to come back for another visit.

I sold my harvest for a very good price and I took the wife on a well-deserved vacation. I never told her about the encounter, for I thought it would scare her and she would want to sale the place and move somewhere else. I will tell you this. I still see the creatures from time to time. The small Bigfoot has grown a lot since the first sighting and they still travel from the back of the fields to the mound in the middle. When I do see them, I just let them be and go on doing what I need to get done.

Thanks for letting me share my story. Its hard to keep a story bottled up and never tell anyone about it. It seems I have relief now that the story is out for others to hear about.

Pete